Merton the MudSKipper

TOP THAT

Licensed exclusively to Top That Publishing Ltd
Tide Mill Way, Woodbridge, Suffolk, IP12 1AP, UK
www.topthatpublishing.com
Copyright © 2014 Tide Mill Media
All rights reserved
2 4 6 8 9 7 5 3
Manufactured in China

Illustrated by Tracey Tucker
Written by Sally Hopgood

ISBN 978-1-78445-375-6

A catalogue record for this book is available from the British Library

'For Tom'

Sally Hopgood

Of all the strange fish in the sea,
Merton was one of the strangest.
His eyes sat on the very top of his head,
and his mouth was on the tip of his chin.

'Boggle eyes!'

'Wibble chin!'

Because he was different,
all the other fish would tease
Merton and call him names.

To escape the teasing, Merton would swim away up to the surface. Here, he discovered that having eyes on top of your head could be very useful. For instance, he could watch the hungry seabirds without them noticing him ...

... and he could watch the crabs scuttling about on the shore.

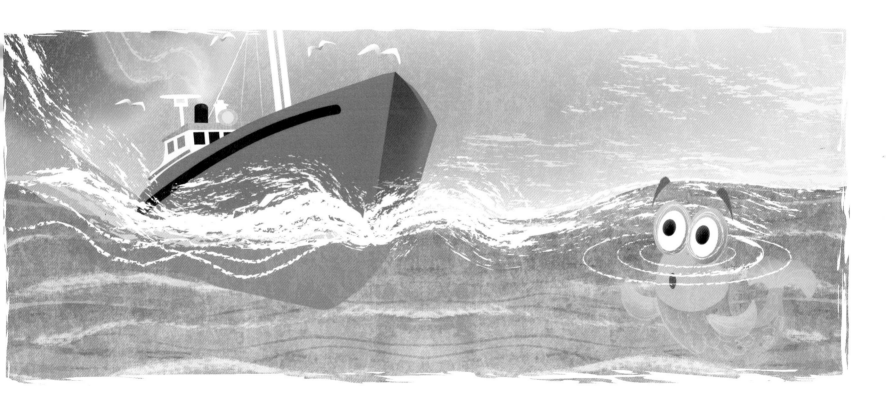

But today, Merton could see a big, smoke-belching monster coming towards him!

Merton called out to the other fish.
'Flee, flee, swim away!'
But, they just laughed at him.

Then, **whooooosh!**

All of the fish
disappeared ...

... except Merton.

Merton swam,

and swam,

and swam,

until he could
swim no further.

Exhausted, he lay in the warm shallows and, despite feeling scared, fell asleep.

Sometime later, Merton awoke with a start.
'Where has the water gone? I can't breathe!' he gasped.

'This way, quick!' said a little crab, waving his pincers.

With several skips, Merton followed the crab
and jumped into a small pool of water.

'Thank you so much,' said Merton to the crab, whose name was Kristoff. 'What happened to the sea?'

Kristoff explained that the sea goes out and comes back in twice every day.

'How will I survive until it comes back?' asked Merton, as the small pool started to dry up.

Luckily, Kristoff had a plan!

'I'll dig you new pools as I feed on the mudflats,' said Kristoff.

'You can skip from pool to pool until the sea comes back.'

Kristoff set to work.

Hopping from pool to pool soon turned into a game.

'Look how well he skips over the mud!'

... and **somersaults,** which impressed all of the crabs nearby.

'What's his name?'

Merton's **skips** and **jumps** became elaborate **twists** ...

'I think it's Merton. Ha, it's Merton the Mudskipper!'

Soon, the sea was back again.
Merton waved goodbye to his new friend.

'I'll come back and visit soon!' he called out.

That night, Merton discovered that the sea had changed. There were very few fish, the coral was destroyed and dark menacing shadows circled over the reef.

'I don't like it here,' said Merton. 'It was much nicer with my friend Kristoff on the shore.'

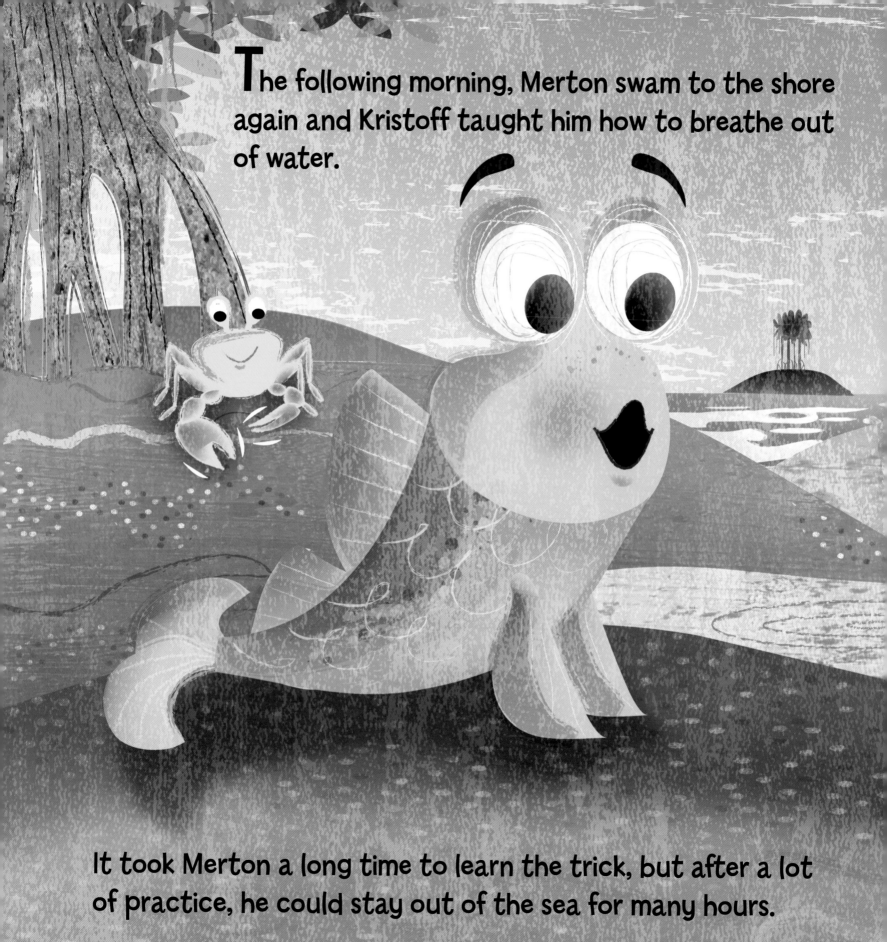

The following morning, Merton swam to the shore again and Kristoff taught him how to breathe out of water.

It took Merton a long time to learn the trick, but after a lot of practice, he could stay out of the sea for many hours.

There was no reason to go back to the scary sea now. Instead, Merton and Kristoff spent their days playing together on the mudflats.

'See you tomorrow!'

Merton even built his home next to Kristoff.

'See you tomorrow!'

As time passed, other mudskippers joined Merton on the mudflats and he taught them how to breathe air.

Merton had learnt that it is good to be different.
Best of all, Merton loved his new friends and home on the mudflats.